TALES FROM THE CRYPT

VOLUME 2

Introduced by the Old Witch

Story adaptations by Eleanor Fremont

Random House 🏠 New York

The stories in this volume first appeared in different form
in *Tales from the Crypt Comic Books* in the following years:

"Fare Tonight, Followed by Increasing Clottiness."
Copyright 1953 by I. C. Publishing Co., Inc.
Copyright renewed 1981 by William M. Gaines, Agent.

"Ghost Ship." Copyright 1950 by I. C. Publishing Co., Inc.
Copyright renewed 1978 by William M. Gaines, Agent.

"A-Corny Story." Copyright 1951 by I. C. Publishing Co., Inc.
Copyright renewed 1979 by William M. Gaines, Agent.

"None but the Lonely Heart." Copyright 1952 by I. C. Publishing Co., Inc.
Copyright renewed 1980 by William M. Gaines, Agent.

"Curse of the Full Moon." Copyright 1949 by I. C. Publishing Co., Inc.
Copyright renewed 1977 by William M. Gaines, Agent.

"Concerto for Violin and Werewolf." Copyright 1954 by I. C. Publishing
Co., Inc. Copyright renewed 1982 by William M. Gaines, Agent.

Library of Congress Cataloging-in-Publication Data
Fremont, Eleanor.   Tales from the crypt / introduced by the
Crypt-Keeper and the Old Witch ; story adaptations by Eleanor Fremont.
    p.   cm.   Adaptation of: Tales from the crypt / William M. Gaines.
SUMMARY: A collection of horror stories, featuring such grisly
characters as a vampire, werewolf, and murderous madman.
ISBN 0-679-81799-9 (v. 1 : pbk.)   ISBN 0-679-81800-6 (v. 2 : pbk.)
1. Horror tales, American.   2. Children's stories, American.
[1. Horror stories.   2. Short stories.]   I. Gaines, William M.   Tales from
the crypt.   II. Title.   PZ7.W4472Tal 1991   [Fic]—dc20   90-23916

CONTENTS

FROM THE OLD WITCH

 *Hey, kiddies, guess what time it is? Dinnertime! And for your icky enjoyment, wonderful Witchy has whomped up a whole cauldronful of foul fare. I've used every repulsive, revolting recipe I can find—so it's time to climb into your highchair, tie on that cute little bib, and dig in. What? You don't <u>like</u> worms? Well, then, try some of the other treats that await you in my cauldron.*

For an appetizer we have a story about a New York cabdriver. Now, that's probably terrifying enough all by itself, but if you don't play your cards right, this particular cabdriver might just take you to the Vampire State Building. So if you like your hors d'oeuvres red—and warm— and sort of liquid, give this story a taste. It's called "Fare Tonight, Followed by Increasing Clottiness."

The first course is another kind of trip entirely—
this one on the high seas. The waves you
encounter there, however, may be waves of nausea,
as you meet the very nasty crew of the "Ghost
Ship."

The third slimy item I'll pull out of my vat for
you is called "A-Corny Story." It's a special gift for
all you tree-huggers out there—a nifty lesson in
bloodcurdling botany.

Now, what's this emerging from the goo in my
bubbling cauldron? Could it be . . . a heart? How
delicious! How appropriate! You see, the next
story is called "None but the Lonely Heart," and
it just might make your own little ticker skip a
beat or two.

And what revolting repast would be complete
without a good gory werewolf tale, I ask you? Not
one of mine, that's for sure. So belly up to the old
cauldron and take a bite out of "Curse of the Full
Moon." Yum, yum.

For dessert we have some musical
accompaniment: a strolling violinist. Isn't that
wonderful? Gee, he's kind of hairy, isn't he? And
he's got such nice, big teeth. Perhaps you recognize
the tune he's playing? It's called "Concerto for
Violin and Werewolf."

Well, I'm sure you'll sleep very well after such a

nutritious meal. So it's off to beddy-bye. I'll tuck you into your iron maiden and sing you a lullaby. How about "Dem Bones"? Or maybe "Scream a Little Scream for Me"?

Nighty-night!

The Old Witch

Well, kiddies, fasten your seat belts. It's going to be a bumpy night. As long as we're out on the town, why don't we hail a cab? How about that one over there? The one with the strange-looking driver? And while we're on our way, I'll tell you a little story called . . .

FARE TONIGHT, FOLLOWED BY INCREASING CLOTTINESS

You slam down the trunk lid of your taxicab and look around. The night is damp and a faint trace of fog drifts in from the bay, chilling you to the bone. You stand there for a moment, shivering. You fumble in your jacket pocket for a cigarette, pull out a half-empty pack, and shake one between your lips. The flame of the match flaring up in the gloom burns your eyes. Even after you've blown it out, its glow still dances before you.

"Hmmph," you mumble to yourself, shrugging your jacket up a little higher around your neck. "Nice night for a murder."

You shuffle around to the front of your cab, swing open the door, and settle inside.

Maybe, you think, you'll cruise the west side tonight.

The fog is a blanket of gray mist on your windshield, so you snap on the wipers. Industrious little fingers whip back and forth, whisking the water away. You peer at the distorted asphalt ahead. The streets are deserted.

"Cripes," you remark to your empty cab, "not a soul around. What a night to try to scrape up a fare!"

Now it has begun to rain. A soft drizzle at first, then heavier and heavier. The water cascades before you, and the industrious little wipers scramble madly back and forth clearing it away, first to one side, then the other.

"Well, that finishes it." You sigh as you peer through the rain. "I'll never get a fare now."

You cruise for a little while longer, searching the sidewalks for a signaling passerby, a homeward-bound customer—but you see no one. You shrug and pull up to a deserted hack stand.

No use wasting gas, you decide. You'll just park here by the subway exit. You shut off the engine and sit back, extracting another butt from your pack. A roar below tells you that a subway train has pulled in. A few seconds later figures pour from the subway exit, their unsmiling faces averted from the rain.

"Taxi? Taxi, lady? Taxi?" you call. They don't even look up.

The subway riders hurry off into the wet gloom. Meanwhile the guy in the newsstand at the corner is trying to unload his night's paper order. "Read all about it!" he shouts. "Another body found! Another murder! Read all about it!"

"Taxi? Taxi?" you continue shouting as the people move past.

Then the rushing shadows are gone. The night and the rain settle down again. You stare across the mirrored sidewalk to the newsstand.

Another murder. Curiosity gets the better of you. You snap open the cab door and dart through the rain to the newsstand.

"Paper, mister?" asks the man, not looking up.

"Yeah," you reply. "Thanks." You put your coins down on the counter and dart back to your cab.

You settle into the driver's seat once more, light up another butt, and open the paper. The headlines scream at you: ANOTHER BODY FOUND!

"'The corpse of a thirty-year-old woman,'" you read, "'was found drained of its blood last night. This is the thirteenth victim to date. . . .'"

Another murder. Thirteen of them now. Each body drained of its blood. You read over the columns of tiny print—the gory details. Suddenly a paragraph catches your eye.

"'A suggestion that a vampire might be responsible for these murders was offered by Dr. Egbert Muller, noted mythologist. Police have rejected this possibility.'"

You shiver. The work of a vampire! You look around uncomfortably, squinting out at the downpour. The rain pounds down on your cab roof, down on the engine hood, down the windshield, in dark torrents.

Suddenly he is beside you, his black overcoat collar turned up, covering the lower part of his face. His black hat brim is turned down, shielding the upper part. Only his eyes glare like firelights from the recesses of their sockets.

"Busy?" he asks, leaning in toward the window.

"No siree!" you answer brightly. "Hop in! Where to?"

He mutters the street and number and slides into the back seat. He carries a briefcase, which he holds on his lap. You start the engine and pull away, grinning. A customer at last.

You glance at him in the mirror. He is looking straight ahead, stone-faced.

"Rotten weather, eh?" you say.

"I hadn't noticed." His answer is curt, almost insulting. It is a brief announcement that he does not care to converse. You shrug and guide your heap through the torrents to the address he's given you.

"All right, stop here," he directs.

"Yes, sir."

The street is in one of the worst neighborhoods in the city. It is a narrow litter-strewn cobblestone alley meshed between sad-faced, starving tenements. Your fare steps out into the downpour. "Wait here for me," he says.

"Yes, sir."

He scurries into a darkened hallway and disappears into its shadows. You shrug, glance at the meter, and settle back to wait. The longer that meter keeps running, the more you get paid.

The rain is letting up now. The street is a black mirror reflecting squalor. Then something in *your* mirror catches your eye. It's his briefcase.

You turn around and stare at the shiny new leather briefcase your customer has left on the back seat. The gold initials pulsate in the light from the street lamp.

"E. M., Ph.D.," you muse. "E. M., Ph.D.

What *is* there about those initials?"

The newspaper rolled up beside you reminds you. "Of course!" you say. "Egbert Muller, the noted mythologist—the man who's trying to convince the police that the murderer is a vampire!"

You pull out your pack of butts, fishing for another cigarette. The pack is empty. You curse. Far down the block, at the corner, a dim light filters through a window, silhouetting the letters painted on it.

"A bar," you mutter. "They'd have a cigarette machine."

You swing from the cab and start down the long dark street. The rain has stopped. A muddy stream of water rushing headlong at the curbside pours down into a foul-smelling sewer, pulling the last traces of rain with it. Above, the clouds are breaking up. And here and there a star blinks through a black hole in the gray cover. It's going to be a nice night after all.

You're almost at the corner when the lights in the bar window disappear and blackness descends. The sign on the door laughs at you, and the laugh echoes over the slick streets and off the grinning faces of the tenements.

"Closed!" you say, staring at the locked door. "Blast it!"

The laugh dies. Silence closes in. Thick, black, frightening silence. Strange. No radio playing? No baby crying? No sounds of the people that live behind the mute tenement facades? Just silence . . .

"No wonder," you think, looking more closely at the buildings. "These tenements are all boarded up. They're deserted."

Then why the bar? What business could a bar do in a condemned-tenement district? You start back to your cab. And then you hear them. At first you think they're echoes of your own, but when you stop, they continue. Footsteps.

Someone's following you.

You quicken your steps. The cab is a million miles away. Behind you the footsteps increase their tempo too. You begin to run. You'll never reach the cab in time!

An open hallway yawns at you. You duck in, cringing in the shadows. A figure hurries by. Black overcoat, black hat. It's him! Your customer! Muller!

You hear his footsteps pounding up the block. In your chest your heart is pounding, too. Then the footsteps stop, and your heart skips a beat. Is he coming back?

You back off into the gloom. The footsteps approach. He stands framed in the hallway entrance, his eyes burning like two white-hot coals.

"You can't escape, my friend!" he gloats. "You're *trapped!*"

His eyes seem to pierce the darkness, seem to search you out of the shadows. Can he see you there? Can his eyes penetrate the night like . . . a bat's? Like a vampire's?

You shriek. You open your quivering lips and you shriek. And you turn and run down the long black corridor, stumbling, getting up, running again.

"It's no use," his steely voice calls to you. "You're trapped. I've caught you!"

"No! No!" you cry.

The cellar door hangs crazily on broken, rusted hinges. Steps lead down into blackness. You lunge through. You've got to escape, you've just got to.

The steps, rotted and decayed, give way beneath your weight, and you tumble into the darkness, screaming.

You struggle to your feet. Above you, your customer peers down through the cellar doorway. He is a black figure against the dim light. "You're trapped," he says, snickering. His laugh echoes loudly through the damp, dark cellar.

Suddenly there are strange sounds about you: creaking noises and deep sighs and flutterings in the dark. The cellar is filled with long evil-looking boxes. No, not boxes at all.

You gasp. They're coffins!

The lids have come alive now, slipping from

the coffins, swinging up, falling back. Gaunt-faced figures, their fanged mouths oozing spittle, rise from their depths.

"No! No! No!" you scream. *"Eeeee-aaaaaahhh!"*

They stumble toward you, shrieking, laughing, reaching out. Vampires!

And then they are upon you, their fangs ripping and tearing at your flesh, their lips closing over your wounds, drawing the life fluid that pours red from them—and you scream. You are helpless under their onslaught. There is nothing else to do but scream . . .

The scream echoes and re-echoes in your ears. You claw at the cold leather seat . . . and open your eyes.

"Huh?" you grunt. "Wha—? Where *am* I?" You are panting.

The rain chatters on your cab roof. People pour from the subway exit. The newsman chants at them: "Read all about it! Another body found! Another murder! Read all about it!"

You're still at the hack stand by the subway exit. The realization dawns on you: you fell asleep. You've been dreaming.

You stare down at the open paper on your lap. His name seems to rise from the blocks of type, magnified, black, and shining.

"Dr. Egbert Muller!" you exclaim. "Why did I dream about him? Why?"

And then he is beside you, his black overcoat pulled up, his black hat brim turned down, and his eyes glaring like firelights.

"Busy?" he asks.

"No siree," you reply. "Hop in! Where to?"

You don't have to look at the initials on the briefcase he is carrying. You know who he is. He slides into the back seat and mutters the street and number. You turn on the motor and pull away.

And all the time you're thinking: "Why did I dream about him? And the vampires—attacking me? What did it all mean?"

Suddenly you know. You know the meaning of your nightmare. And you know what you must do.

"This isn't the way!" says Muller tightly, looking out the window.

"It's a shortcut, Dr. Muller," you explain. You can see his eyes in the rearview mirror.

You stop the cab. It's one of the worst neighborhoods in the city. The neighborhood you dreamed about.

You step out of the cab and open the door to the back seat, gesturing for Muller to get out.

"You—you know me?" he asks, looking frightened.

"Yes, Doctor. Get out."

It's clear now. The whole dream is clear. Dr. Egbert Muller is a threat to you. That's why you dreamed of him following you . . . tracking you down . . .

"My—my briefcase!" he stammers. "I left it on the seat!"

"You won't need it, Doc," you snarl.

And the vampires, the ones that attacked you in the cellar. Dr. Muller knows about vampires. All about them. Sooner or later he'd convince the police . . .

"Where are you taking me?" he dithers as you shove him into the entranceway of an abandoned building. "This hallway—it's so dark!"

It would be his vast knowledge of vampires

that would mean your ultimate death. The dream made sense. The dream was a warning . . .

"Who *are* you?" he asks, stark terror in his eyes. "Who—oh, no! No! No! *My god!*"

"Yes, Doctor," you say. Your bared fangs are clearly visible now. "Yes."

He struggles, but you are strong. You bend over him and sink your fangs into his soft white neck, drawing in the thick red life fluid that you must have.

And when the last drop is gone, you fling his lifeless body down the rotted cellar steps to join the others. Only *thirteen* victims? Hah! Wait till they find the *rest* down there!

As dawn breaks, you open the trunk of your cab and crawl in onto the thin layer of soil.

"I'd—ho-hum—better get a good day's rest today," you say with a yawn, feeling full and satisfied. "Imagine, a vampire falling asleep at *night!* And *dreaming,* yet. . . ."

Well, gotta go. In a hurry. Taxi! Oh, taxi!

Rats. How come you can never get one when you need one?

Well, my little fiends, perhaps taxi rides aren't quite to your taste. Perhaps you'd like to take a very different sort of ride—a trip on a . . .

GHOST SHIP

My story begins high over the Atlantic Ocean, a few hundred miles north of Bermuda. A tiny plane is winging its way through a cloudless sky. Inside sits a young couple.

"Oh, darling!" rhapsodizes the young woman. "What a wonderful way to begin our honeymoon . . . flying to Bermuda!"

"I thought you'd like it, sweetheart," he replies, keeping his eyes on the instruments and his hands on the controls.

"Like it! I *love* it!" she says. "It's like a fairyland with the beautiful blue of the ocean far below . . ."

"Uh-oh," he says, peering into the distance. "Looks like a fog bank coming in over the horizon."

Swiftly the small plane speeds toward the menacing fog bank.

"I'll try to go up over it, Carol," explains the self-assured young pilot.

"Can't we avoid it—go around it?" she asks.

"No, it would take us too far off our course," he says, furrowing his brow. "And my gas supply might not last. No, I'll take her up over it."

The drone of the motors grows louder as Don's plane strains to climb above the blanket of fog.

"I don't think we're going to make it, Carol," he says through clenched teeth. "It's too much for her." There is a loud sputtering sound from the engines as they strain and finally stall.

"The motors conked out! We're going down!" he screams.

"Don!" she shrieks, clutching her new husband. "We'll be killed!"

Down, down through the thick pea-soup fog the plane and its two occupants drop. And then—an opening in the fog!

"I'm going to try to put her down on the

water!" he shouts. "Fasten your safety belt, Carol!"

She pulls the belt tight around her slim waist and hangs on to her husband.

Straining for a glimpse of the ocean as the crippled plane rushes toward it, Don peers into the thick fog. Suddenly he sees through the opening and frantically pulls up on the controls. With a huge splash the plane hits the water.

"Quickly, Carol! Give me your hand!" he orders as they climb out onto the top of the plane. "The cabin may fill up with water!"

"Don—the life raft!" she cries. "Don't we have one?"

"That's right! I'll go back and get it, darling!"

"Hurry, Don, my love!" she says. "We're sinking fast!"

Frantically Don climbs back down into the cabin and emerges with the precious life raft, which he speedily inflates. As they pull away from the wreckage, the plane turns tail up and sinks.

"Oh, darn," says the handsome young man.

For hours they float in the dense fog, straining their eyes and ears for a sign of a ship.

"Don!" says the young wife. "We have no water, no food, nothing! We won't be able to last very long!" She pulls her jacket a little more closely around her shoulders.

"Don't worry, Carol," says Don bravely. "The fog will lift, and then a ship or a plane will spot us."

But the fog does not lift. It remains for one day and then for two. Carol and Don, tired and weak from hunger and thirst, drift aimlessly about in the little rubber raft, listening—and looking—in vain.

Then a strange noise comes to them through the fog: a creaking sound of old timbers rotted and worn, straining and grating against one another.

"Do you hear that, Don?" says Carol.

"Yes, my darling," he says. "It sounds like—*look!*"

Before them out of the gloom rises the enormous hulk of a great ship, or what's left of one. The sails hang in rags on the splintered masts, and the hull is rotted and black.

"It's a ship!" says Carol. "An old sailing vessel!"

"All decayed," adds Don. "It's a wonder it's afloat!"

Don rises to his knees in the boat, dusting off his leather jacket. "Let's go aboard, Carol," he says.

"No, Don," she says. "I'm *afraid!* There's something strange about it!"

"But Carol, my dearest," he says, "if this fog hangs on much longer, we'll die of thirst. Maybe there's food and water aboard."

"Look, Don!" says Carol, pointing up. "Isn't that a light? See? There *is* someone on board."

"Hello!" calls Don. "Hello up there!"

"That's funny," says Carol. "There's no answer."

Then Don spots a rope ladder on the side of the ship. "Come on, my sweetest," he says. "We'll tie up the raft and climb aboard."

Carefully they climb the fraying ladder. Carol's spike heels catch in the rope, but she keeps climbing. At last Don reaches the top of the ladder and turns to help his new wife up onto the deck.

"Thanks, dear," she says, out of breath. "I—*what's that?*"

"*What? Where?*" he says.

"Look, Don! A skeleton! Lashed to the helm!"

"Good lord!" he cries. There it is, all right. The tattered remnants of a sailor's clothes cling to the bony apparition, which is tied securely by both wrists to the huge wooden helm of the ship.

"And look!" gasps Carol. "There's one hanging from the yardarm!"

Don shudders. "I—I don't understand!"

"Look, darling," says Carol. "I was right! There *is* a light in the cabin!"

"C'mon," says Don bravely. "Let's take a look."

They peer through the dirty window into the gloom of the cabin below the deck. "There's someone down there," whispers Carol.

Sure enough, there is a figure sitting at a wooden table reading a book. The figure is shrouded in a hooded garment; its face is impossible to see.

The frightened couple make their way down the dark stairs to the cabin and knock on the door. There is no answer. Don lifts the latch and the door squeaks open.

"Why, there's no one here now!" he says in surprise.

"Don!" says Carol, grabbing her husband's arm. "I'm afraid! Let's go back to the raft!"

"Nonsense," says Don. "We probably scared whoever it was away. Look, here's the book he was reading!"

They hold it up in the dim light. "It looks like a ship's log!" Carol says.

"Great Scott!" exclaims Don. "The last entry is dated January 6, 1854!"

"Go back a bit and read what happened up to that day, Don," suggests Carol.

Don begins reading aloud. " 'October 17, 1853: Today seized the British frigate *Golden Star,* killing all hands aboard and capturing booty of jewels and gold coin. The men are dissatisfied with the split, I taking almost half for myself. Captain Henry Dragoon.' "

"Why, then, this was a *pirate vessel,*" says Carol. "And Dragoon was its captain!"

"Yes," says Don, still reading. "But listen to *this:* 'October 27, 1853: A mutiny is stirring, led by one of the men, Charles Groggins. I fear for the lives of myself and my mate. Captain Henry Dragoon.' "

Carol and Don can just picture the scene on the ship in 1853: the rough, hairy pirates, gold rings in their ears, pounding their fists into their hands. "Let's string them up, the cheats," the pirates would be saying. "Then the whole treasure will be ours."

Carol gives a little shudder as Don continues reading. " 'October 29, 1853: They have killed the other officers and I myself remain, locked in this cabin. I can hear them outside, ready to break down the door. This will probably be my last entry in the log. The battering is already shattering the door panels, and I—' It ends abruptly!" says Don. "They probably killed him!"

"Look!" says Carol. "On the next page— another entry in a *different* handwriting!"

Don keeps reading. " 'October 30, 1853: Today, as the new captain of this vessel, I ordered Henry Dragoon to walk the plank. In his parting words he cursed us and swore revenge. "Mark my words!" he said. "I will return to command this vessel! Death to all of you will be my revenge!" The men had no sympathy for him. "Go on, stop your chattering and take your final step," they shouted. The men laughed and he disappeared into the briny sea. I immediately set about to find the share of the treasure *he* had taken, but to no avail. It had vanished. "What means this, Groggins?" the men asked me angrily. "It is the truth, men," I could only reply. "The booty is nowhere in the cabin." The men do not like this bad news. Charles Groggins.' "

Don keeps reading the log, eager to see

what happened to Groggins and the other men. "'November 13, 1853,'" he reads. "'The men have begun to quarrel among themselves. They do not trust me. They believe that I have taken the captain's share of the treasure for myself, and now they are talking about stringing me up.'"

Carol shudders. "Ooh, it's all so horrible, Don," she says. "What comes next?"

"'November 15, 1853,'" Don continues. "'The men have given me until today to produce the captain's share of the booty. I cannot find it. All my pleading has been in vain. They are at the door now. I fear that my hours are numbered! Charles Groggins.' And that," says Don, "is the last entry in his writing."

"Who continues it, Don?" asks his wife.

"Let's see," says Don. "The next entry is November 16, 1853: 'A thorough search of the cabin has not produced the treasure. Charles Groggins's body swings from the highest yardarm, and I am taking it upon myself to continue this log. John Bates.'

"'December 5, 1853: There has been a dead calm for three weeks now. The sails are slack, and there is no wind. The ship has slowly drifted into a great morass of seaweed, and we are held fast by millions of entwining plants. Some of the men, believing we will never break loose from the seaweed even if we do get a breeze, want to take to the small boats with what is left of the stores and the water. Others feel that this would be folly and would lead to death by exposure and starvation.'

" 'December 18, 1853: After much discussion, most of the men took their shares of the stores and left the ship in the small boats. There are but a few of us left. This morning Johnson saw an albatross. Carter wanted to kill the great bird, assuring us of a bit of food, but I reminded him that it is well known to be bad luck to kill an albatross.'

" 'January 3, 1854: My hand can hardly hold the plume. I am weak with hunger. Our food and water ran out four days ago and still the albatross hovers over us, its screeching driving us out of our minds. Just as Carter resolved to kill it, I felt a breeze and saw blessed storm clouds on the horizon.'

" 'January 4, 1854: The storm hit last night

at eight bells. Our sails are full set, but this cursed seaweed holds us fast. Already the ship, battered by the stormy sea, is beginning to crack and strain. Johnson has tied himself to the helm so that he may steer us out should we break loose. The albatross has gone.'

"'January 5, 1854: Carter has strangled while tying a sail on the mizzenmast, and he hangs like a banner in the wind. Johnson is still lashed to the helm, and I sit here in the cabin. The water is beginning to fill the hold. We are sinking fast. I will finish this entry and take to the sea. It is my last hope. John Bates.'"

Carol pulls her jacket a little tighter around her shoulders. "Is that all, Don?" she asks in a quavering voice.

"No," says Don. "There's this last entry, dated January 6, 1854. It says, 'The ship is mine again! I will sail it into eternity! Captain Henry Dragoon.' This is crazy, Carol! The last entry is in Dragoon's handwriting, too!"

"Listen. Did you hear that?" says Carol. "A foghorn!"

The couple rush out to the deck of the strange vessel. Through the gloom of the fog the lights of a tanker come toward them. "A ship, Don! We're saved!" shouts Carol joyously.

"Ahoy! Ahoy, there!" yells Don at the top of his lungs.

"They don't hear us! They're coming right *at* us!"

"They're going to ram us!"

The sharp prow of the enormous gray tanker is bearing down fast on them now. Clearly it has not seen the pirate ship. Carol and Don race to the end of the deck in fear of their lives. The tanker will break the ship in half! It is upon them now!

Soundlessly, without so much as a ripple, the tanker slices right through the center of the pirate ship—*as if it weren't even there.*

"Good lord!" exclaims Don.

And then the tanker is past. "I . . . I . . . I think I'm going to faint," says Carol, leaning against her husband.

"C'mon, Carol! We've got to get to our life raft!"

Quickly Don and Carol climb down the side of the old rotted ship into their raft. They paddle furiously, calling after the tanker, "Help! Ahoy! Help!"

"Listen!" comes a shout from the deck of the tanker.

"Man overboard!" comes another cry. They've been heard!

Once on board the tanker they are fed and made comfortable. Then Don and Carol tell their fantastic story. The captain and seamen are sympathetic and friendly but clearly don't believe the couple's tale.

"Utter nonsense," scoffs the captain. "An illusion caused by exposure and starvation."

"*Our* ship passed right *through* it, you say?" The first mate, so modern and down-to-earth, chuckles. "I think you both need rest—plenty of rest!"

And Carol and Don just look at each other.

Well, that's the story. Pretty strange, isn't it? What do you think happened? Was it all in their minds . . . or did Don and Carol actually sail on a ghost ship? Or are you too seasick to care? Come to think of it, you do look a little green around the gills, kiddies. Oh, well. The next story takes place on dry land, so maybe you'll do a little better. But don't bet on it. . . .

Well, my little pretties, are you ready for story number tree? It's about a guy who didn't act his age. You'll shudder over this one, even though it's called . . .

A-CORNY STORY

Arnold Everette strode down the aisle between the rows of desks that lined his office, glancing from one to the other. He smiled to himself as he noted the occupant of each. Yes, things were working out fine. There was only one man left, one man to get rid of: Old Man Pietro.

Arnold stopped before the graying, aged Carlo Pietro's desk and looked down at the gaunt figure.

"Er, will you see me in my office, Mr. Pietro? Say, in ten minutes?"

Carlo Pietro looked up through his thick glasses at his boss. Everette was dressed in an expensive suit with a fancy silk tie and hand-kerchief to match. He had a deep tan and sparkling white teeth. The man was fairly bursting with youth and health.

"Yes, sir," said the old man, squinting through his glasses and gathering up a pile of papers on his desk. "I'll be right there."

Arnold returned to his luxurious private office and waited impatiently for Pietro's knock. After a while it came—two timid raps.

"Come in!" said Arnold heartily.

"You . . . wanted to see me, Mr. Everette?" faltered Carlo Pietro.

"Yes, Mr. Pietro! Come in! Sit down!" Arnold's smile was wide, and his teeth twinkled.

The wrinkled old man sat down nervously. Arnold studied him, noting his trembling, bony hands and his grim, skull-like face.

"I've instructed the cashier to issue you a check for two weeks' pay in advance, Mr. Pietro," said Arnold, smiling. "I'm sorry, but I'm forced to let you go."

"But—why, sir?" asked Pietro, stricken. "Did I do something wrong?"

"No. Pietro." Arnold chuckled. "It's not that. It's just that you're too old! I want only young men working for Everette and Son!"

"But Mr. Everette!" protested Pietro. "I've

been here for twenty years! I worked for your father before you!"

"That doesn't matter now," said Arnold, putting a friendly arm around Pietro. "My father is dead. There is no room for sentiment in business. I want no old men working for me. They're slow. They tire easily."

"Please!" begged Pietro. "I have no place to go . . . no one to turn to!"

"You don't have a family, Carlo?"

"No. They are all back in Haiti. I left them twenty-five years ago, when I came to work in America."

"Well, why not go back to them? A man your age should retire anyway!"

"Perhaps you are right," said Pietro sadly. "I only hope that when you are old, you are not treated this way."

Arnold turned away from the wretched old man and glanced into the mirror. Except for a few worry lines across his forehead, he scarcely looked his thirty-five years. "Don't worry, Carlo," he said, studying his handsome face in the mirror. "I'll make sure I'm not dependent on anyone when that time comes."

"Some of us are not as fortunate," said Pietro. "You do not have to fear old age."

"Not with *my* dough, Carlo." Arnold laughed. "But I'm a busy man. You can pick up your check on the way out. Good day."

"Good-bye, Mr. Everette. Perhaps your love of youth—and contempt for old age—will change in the future. We will see."

Carlo Pietro shuffled out of the offices of Everette and Son and never returned. Arnold hired a young man to take his place, and Carlo was soon forgotten.

But several weeks later, in Haiti, there was a brief business transaction between a witch doctor and old Carlo Pietro.

"What do you want with voodoo, old man?" the witch doctor asked him. "Why do you come to see me?"

"I want something," said Pietro, "for one who loves youth too much. I want to teach him a lesson. . . ."

Two months went by. Arnold Everette got richer and richer, and his suits got more and more expensive. His office was filled with eager young employees who worked hard to increase the wealth of Everette and Son.

One day a crate arrived at the home of Arnold Everette. He surveyed it on the rear terrace of his palatial estate, overlooking the formal, sculptured gardens.

"What in the world could it be, Jeeves?" he asked his butler. "Is there a return address?"

"Yes, sir," said Jeeves. "It comes from Haiti. A Carlo Pietro sent it."

The crate stood about seven feet high. Arnold scowled at it. "Pietro, eh? Well, we might as well open it and see what it is."

Jeeves pried the sides of the crate loose with a crowbar, and they fell away.

"Why, look at that, sir!" he said in amazement. "It's a small tree. How quaint! Look how gnarled and twisted it is!"

"There's a note hanging on one of its branches," observed Arnold. He pulled off the note and read:

Dear Mr. Everette:
In my native land this tree is worshipped by the uneducated. They believe that it can ward off old age. Knowing how much you despise that inevitable state, I send this variety of oak to you. Perhaps it will help.

"Sarcastic old codger," Arnold muttered, crumpling the note and throwing it aside.

"What shall we do with it, sir?" asked Jeeves.

"How in blazes should *I* know?" snapped Arnold. "Plant it, I guess. It's an interesting type of tree, in any case. Yes, plant it."

And so while Arnold Everette watched, his servant dug a hole near the garden wall and planted the weird gnarled dwarf tree.

"That's a good spot for it," said Arnold. "I can't see it from the house, so I won't be reminded of the ugly thing!"

A week went by. The burden of work that

had grown so heavy on Arnold seemed lighter somehow. Arnold moved about briskly and began to feel more energetic.

"Good day, Mr. Everette!" Jeeves would say as his boss bounced down the stairs two at a time. "You're looking well this morning!"

"I *feel* well this morning!" Arnold would reply heartily.

Arnold found a desire to play golf again, something he hadn't done for years. Not only was he enjoying it, he was playing wonderfully. He hadn't made shots like this since he was thirty.

Even his visits to nightclubs and theaters with old flames grew more frequent. "Oh, Arnold," his old girlfriend Helen murmured into his ear one night at an expensive supper club. "You're such a fantastic dancer! This brings back old memories, doesn't it?"

"Not so old, Helen," he answered. "Remember: think young, feel young!" And he turned her around and dipped her back, laughing.

Then one morning Arnold saw something odd when he looked into the mirror. "That's funny," he said to himself. "I used to have wrinkles on my forehead and under my eyes. Now they're gone!"

He shrugged and got dressed.

He was feeling so energetic that morning, he decided to walk to the train station. As he walked out past the garden wall, he noticed the tree.

"Hey, even the tree Pietro sent me looks nicer," he thought. "Doesn't seem as crooked and gnarled anymore. And the leaves look *greener!*"

Arnold smiled and walked on past. Life certainly was bright and cheerful lately. Probably being surrounded by young people at the office did it.

Then a few days later Arnold was again looking into the bathroom mirror. "Hmmm," he mused, feeling his face with his hand. "Doesn't look bad this morning. Think I can squeeze by without a shave today." He got dressed, glad to skip that part of his morning routine.

Arnold was whistling a merry tune as he neared the garden wall after breakfast. But the tune died to a rush of air through his lips as he spied the tree. "Strange," he said to himself.

"The tree seems to be straightening up. It looks
. . . different! Almost . . . younger!"

The next morning Arnold didn't have to
shave again. Or the following morning, for that
matter. Arnold looked into the mirror, the full
force of the shock dawning on him. "Good
lord! My beard! *It's stopped growing!*"

Arnold didn't go to the office one day. He'd
meant to, but a strange desire took hold of him.
The afternoon found him in the bleachers along
with hundreds of teenagers, cheering for the

home team. "C'mon, Pee-Wee!" he screamed. "Slam it, kid! You can do it!"

In fact, Arnold never went to the office again. Somehow he'd suddenly lost interest.

He was more interested in the old swimming hole. "Ah, this is the life," he said, diving in at midday. "Just like when I was a kid!"

Except for the curious fact that his beard had stopped growing and his wrinkles had vanished, Arnold had not noticed the horrible change that was taking place. It wasn't until his tailor exploded that he realized something was wrong.

"Sacre Dieu!" exclaimed Jacques as he fitted the newly made suit onto Arnold's shoul-

ders. "It fits like a bag! Impossible! Your measurements cannot have changed so much!"

"Changed?" said Arnold in a voice that cracked. "How? I . . . I don't understand!"

And one day Jeeves announced that he was leaving. "I'll find employment elsewhere, sir," he said. "Your actions lately . . . er . . . force me to resign. You've been behaving like an adolescent!"

"An—an adolescent?" said Arnold, scratching his head. "Golly! I don't get it, Jeeves! Aw, c'mon, hang around!" He bounced a tennis ball against the living room wall, sulking.

"Really, sir!" said Jeeves, closing the door.

After Jeeves left, Arnold locked himself into the house. He was forced to search through old trunks in the attic for clothes to wear—child's clothes, long since packed away.

"Oh, look!" he cried, peering into a dusty trunk. "My old electric trains! Gee, I wonder if they still work!"

Arnold spent the next three days playing on the floor with his electric trains. He found a big box of chocolate cupcakes in the closet and a big container of milk in the refrigerator, and that's what he ate. He was very happy.

One day as Arnold scampered about the garden, his soccer ball rolled over to the wall. It stopped before a young queerly shaped tree, just a sapling.

"Gee! That tree!" said Arnold in his squeaky little boy's voice. "It . . . it means something, but I . . . I can't remember what!"

It was, of course, the gnarled, crooked old tree that Carlo Pietro had sent not that long ago. Now it stood firm and straight, reaching toward the sunlight. Arnold studied it for a moment, scratched his mop of unkempt hair, and then skipped away. "Oh, well." He laughed. "Another time! Now I've got to go play with my soldiers!"

The next morning Arnold tumbled out of bed onto the floor. He tried to get up, but something was wrong. His short stubby legs wouldn't respond. All that day he crawled around the house, playing. "Bwocks!" he cooed, stacking up his alphabet blocks. "Nice bwocks! Uh-oh! All faw down!"

Near the garden wall the baby that Arnold

Everette had become crawled after an interesting insect. He stopped before a young green
shoot sprouting from the soft, rich earth.
"Pwetty fwower," he babbled. "Nice pwetty
fwower."

That night the otherwise deserted house of
Arnold Everette was filled with the squalling
howls of a hungry infant crying for its bottle.

Toward morning the screams had changed
to the faint gurgles and cries of a newborn
babe.

And soon even those cries died away. As the
morning sun streamed over the garden wall, a

golden ray shot down toward the spot where Arnold Everette several months before had Carlo Pietro's gnarled and crooked tree planted. And there on a bare spot of black earth lay a single object: an acorn.

Well, I hope you seed da point of this weird little tale! Which is worse? Growing old or growing young? Arnold can't help you. But next time somebody says "Aw, grow up!" to you, I think you better take them seriously . . . don't you?

*Well, my dear ones, your hostess in the haunt of fear is ready to rustle up another revolting recipe for you. So creep in! Tie your dribble napkins around your scrawny necks . . . fasten your drool cups . . . and I'll* dish out a tale of terror called:

NONE BUT THE LONELY HEART

It had always been easy for Howard. After all, he *was* rather good-looking, in a mature sort of way. At least *he* thought so. Old maids and widows were attracted to him. Of course, the photos he sent them were especially good ones.

Howard's constant companion was his German shepherd dog, King. The dog would lie at Howard's feet, and Howard would chat with him.

"Heh, heh," Howard said, chuckling, one day as he went through the mail. "Listen to this, King: 'Dear Howard, I received your picture along with your delightfully written letter today. You look very nice! Enclosed is my photo. I'm sorry that it isn't a recent shot. It was taken two years ago.'"

Howard patted his dog's head and smiled. "Well, she's sent us her picture, boy. Shall we brace ourselves and take a look?"

He lifted the picture from the envelope and gasped. "Why, she's *beautiful*, King!"

Indeed, Howard's newest proposed victim *was* beautiful. She had long, curly raven-black hair, skin like sweet cream, and lips as red as rubies. Howard studied the photo thoughtfully. "You know, King, with a woman like this, I might decide to wind up this racket and settle down for good," he mused.

Howard sat back, the picture in his lap, and lit his pipe. The smoke curled up lazily, thinning as it drifted toward the ceiling. "Remember the first picture we ever got, King?" he said. "Let's see . . . it was almost seven years ago. What *was* her name? Oh, yes! Matilda. Matilda Filby.

"We got her name from a lonely-hearts club list, remember? That was back when I first decided to start this little 'love-for-money' game. After a couple of warm letters crossed, her photo came: 'Whew! What a face!' I said to you, King, remember? 'Look at this! How could I ever love anyone so ugly?' "

The dog looked up at Howard and yawned.

"But she had money, didn't she, King? Remember? She wrote, describing her house and all its furnishings. 'She's rich, King,' I said. 'She's got loot. And she lives alone! Maybe . . . maybe looks aren't everything.' But I choked when I said it, didn't I?

"So we took the plunge, eh, boy? We wrote passionate missives of love and finally proposed. And she accepted! So we pawned my watch, bought a new suit of clothes and a ticket, and we went.

" 'Howard, dear one!' she said as she opened the door. And I said, 'Matilda! My pet!' I was trying hard not to turn green, wasn't I, King?"

The dog just blinked at Howard.

"How long was it after our wedding, King? Six months? Not much more. Poor Matilda. She never even knew we'd loosened the top cellar stair. She certainly screamed as she went down, didn't she?

"But the fall didn't kill her, did it? We had to go down and finish the job. Messy business. . . .

"How much did we make on that deal, King?" he said thoughtfully, drawing on his pipe. "Let's see. We sold the house for fifty thousand, and . . . oh, yes! All told, about seventy grand! Of course, I had to explain to the neighbors that it was just too painful for me to stay there with all those memories. They were so sad to see 'Mr. Crown' go."

Howard laughed with pleasure at the thought of it.

"So we moved on, eh, King? And about three months later, we contacted our second victim. She'd advertised in a personal column,

hadn't she? Yep! It began again. I remember what I said to you when her picture came: 'Well, at least she's better than the last one, eh, King? Aren't there any *pretty* widows?'

"It took us six months of ardent love-making via the United States mail to convince *that* one, huh, King? What was her name? Oh, yes: Ephie. Dear Ephie. She looked like a Sherman tank.

"We didn't waste much time with *her,* eh, King? She wasn't as wealthy as we thought. Sometimes it's hard to tell, isn't it? And you can't very well ask! How long did Ephie last before she fell from her apartment window? The fresh-air fiend! Heh, heh. It was so easy to push her. She had jewelry, though. How much did we get? Only five grand or so, wasn't it?

"Of course, I had to explain to the neighbors about how the apartment was, well, so big and empty now. 'Sorry to see you go, Mr. Prince,' they said.

"Number three answered *our* ad, eh, King?" Howard continued. "She was the worst of the lot. Two hundred pounds, at least. And those glasses! And that mole! But she had real estate out in Oklahoma. So off I went.

"'Howard! Dearest!' she said when I got off the train.

"'Luella, my love!' I barely managed to choke out."

Howard scratched King's head, reminiscing. "That job was the cleverest, I must admit. Remember? I made sure to leave you home that day we went driving.

"'Be careful, Howard!' I can still hear her shrieking. 'There's a sharp drop on this turn! You ... you ... *Howard! Where are you going?*'

"'Good-bye, Luella,' I said to her. I leaped from the car just as it went over the cliff. Oh, you should have been there, King! You'd have been proud of me. And what a sight! The car going over and over ... down, down, down ...

"That real estate brought us twenty thousand, King. But what a mistake it was to sell it! They found oil there later! Of all the luck! Oh, well. We made up for it on number four. Remember her? Veronica. Looked like a prune.

"The factory that Veronica's first husband had left her was worth a small fortune. Chemicals. It spelled her own undoing, eh, King? Remember how I learned about that nontraceable poison? I can still see her hacking and turning green. 'Howard! That coffee!' she gasped. 'I—I . . .'

" 'Yes, Veronica? What about it?' I replied mildly.

"Poor Veronica. The poison made her go into such painful convulsions before she died. The two hundred thousand dollars wasn't painful at all, though, was it, King?

" 'You're sure you want to sell, Mr. Royal?' the real-estate man asked me. 'After all—'

" 'Yes, Mr. Bibbs,' I replied sadly. 'I'd rather. I . . . I couldn't go on without . . . *her.*' "

Howard stroked his dog absently, remembering all the good times.

"How many were there altogether, King? Seven? Yes! Seven! Why, we could have retired easily with the fortune we'd made from them. But then we read *this* ad—Janet's ad.

"Remember what it said, King? 'Lonely woman desires correspondence with refined gentleman.'

"We couldn't resist, could we, King? We *had* to write! And then her answer came: 'Dear Mr. Throne, Your letter arrived today, and I read it with much interest. You sound very cultured and well traveled. I would enjoy corresponding with you.' It was signed 'Janet Lane.'"

Howard put his pipe down and smiled. He shuffled through a sheaf of papers.

"So we started writing, eh, King? Let's see! Here's her second letter.

"'Dear Howard,'" he read. "'If I may be so bold, I reside in a sturdily built stone house. The property is very large, almost twelve acres, and very well kept. But for a woman like me,

CAN'T YOU *SEE* HER, KING? THIS *RAVISHING WOMAN* LIVING ALONE ON THIS *PALATIAL ESTATE* IN A *HUGE FIELDSTONE HOUSE!* WHY... IT SOUNDS ALMOST *TOO GOOD TO BE TRUE...*

who is completely alone, life can be very hard. Your letters are a great comfort.'"

Howard sprang to his feet in his excitement. "Can't you see her, King? This ravishing woman living alone on a palatial estate in a huge fieldstone house? Why, it sounds almost too good to be true!"

He pulled out another letter from the sheaf, pacing feverishly now. "Listen to *this* one," he said. "'Marble floors! Furnished in exquisite taste! Hard woods! Bronze trims! Satin draperies! Stained-glass windows!'" A picture of a palace fit for an emperor floated through Howard's mind.

"King, m'boy," he said, "I think it's time that you and I were settling down. We're not getting any younger, you know. And if Janet"—he picked up the photograph of the ravishing young woman—"if Janet looks like *this*, I think we've found the right one this time! Why, you'll have that big estate to romp around in . . . with the wrought-iron gates! And the gardeners! And trees . . . and flowers . . . and a big stone house . . ."

Howard snatched up a pen. "I'm going to propose to her, King! She speaks of how lonely she is. And she has my picture! Maybe ... maybe she'll say yes!"

Three days later Janet's answer came.

"She's accepted, King!" Howard crowed. King was so excited he jumped on Howard and barked. "She'll marry me, King! Oh, I wouldn't let myself hope—but now I'm so happy!"

Howard packed his bags, talking to King the whole time. "No more wandering around for us, boy! No more aliases. No more false lovemaking! We're settling down—for good!"

Howard sent a telegram ahead, announcing his expected arrival date, and he and King set out by car for Janet's home. He drove all day and through the evening, not even stopping to eat.

"Only fifty more miles, boy!" he said. "We'll be there before midnight!"

When they got to Janet Lane's town, Howard spotted a policeman and pulled over to check her address.

"Bayberry Road?" said the cop. "Well, it's straight on south about two miles. You can't miss it." He squinted, trying to see Howard's piece of paper. "What number was that you wanted?" he asked.

"That's all right, officer," said Howard. "I'll find it. Thanks."

Bayberry Road was a long, narrow tree-lined lane off the main highway. There were few houses along it. Finally he spotted the gate.

"There it is, King! We're here!"

As Howard's car swung in at the gate, his headlights fell across . . .

"*What the—?*" Howard gasped.

The letters were rusted and old, but very clear: CEMETERY.

King began to whine softly.

"Steady, boy! Steady! We must have made a mistake!" said Howard, breathing heavily.

Suddenly the car door swung open. King yelped.

"Good lord!" cried Howard. Leaning into the car was a woman—or what was left of one.

The rotted, decayed thing grinned as it reached toward Howard. Its flesh crawled with the slime of death. "Howard . . . Daa-a-a-r-ling!" it breathed.

"Janet! No! No!" Howard shrieked.

King leaped from the car, howling. The thing closed its bony fingers around Howard's wrist in a viselike grip and dragged him from the car toward the open mausoleum.

"I'm sorry I didn't have a more recent snap-

shot, my dear," it rasped hoarsely. "Aren't the grounds just as I described them?"

The female-thing dragged the screaming man into the satin-draped mausoleum with the stained-glass window . . . across the marble floor, and into the hardwood, bronze-trimmed coffin. And all the while, as it closed the lid, it kept murmuring, spewing its foul-smelling breath upon Howard's terror-stricken face, "It's been *so* lonely here, my dear! But now that's all over!"

Hee, hee! What a love affair, eh, kiddies? "All over now" is right—for Howie, that is! Oh, by the way, in case you're wondering what happened to King, rest your fiendish minds! Janet had a lovely dog—named Queenie!

So watch your mail closely, children. And if you get any love letters signed JANET or HOWIE, well, don't send them along to me! My love life is quite horrible enough, thank you!

 *In the dense forests of Eastern Europe there grows a wild plant called wolfsbane. Legend has it that any human who comes into contact with its thorns will become a werewolf, and suffer the . . .*

CURSE OF THE FULL MOON

It is the night of the full moon. The buildings of Gotham are steeped in a drenching rain, and a heavy fog blankets the city, forming eerie patterns in the night.

Between lightning flashes a figure runs the length of a street, darts to the doorway of a building, and frantically hammers on the door. He waits nervously. . . . Nervously, because tonight . . . tonight is the night of the full moon.

At last the door opens. "Yes?" says the handsome, well-dressed man who lives in the safe, warm apartment. "What can I . . . *Ralph!* What on earth . . . ?"

The desperate visitor grabs the surprised man by the lapels. His trench coat is dripping wet. "George! George, you've got to help me!"

pleads the newcomer. "Tonight ... the full moon, George! I'm—I'm afraid! You're a psychiatrist, George. You can help me!"

"Great Scott, man," says George, helping the wild-eyed Ralph out of his wet coat. "Stop that babbling. Get these wet things off first, and then you can tell me all about it."

"Yes, George, yes," says Ralph, relieved. "You're my best friend. I can tell you."

"There," says George soothingly, helping Ralph to lie down on the couch that is usually reserved for George's patients. "Now, just lie back and relax. Relax, and tell me what's frightened you so."

"Yes, yes, relax," says Ralph. "I must compose myself! George, you remember our tour of Europe, don't you?"

"Of course," replies George.

"Remember how we stopped off at that little village in Hungary? We stayed several days, once going for a walk in the forest. Remember?"

"Yes, I remember," says George.

"We were standing there, breathing the forest air," says Ralph. 'A day like this makes you feel glad you're alive, eh, Ralph?' you said.

"'It sure does,' I started to reply, but then I stopped. I said, 'Ouch!' Remember that, George?"

"Yes, I do," says George. "I asked you what had happened."

"That's right," says Ralph. "And I said, 'Oh, it's nothing. I just scratched myself on one of the branches of this bush. Nothing serious, though. A little iodine will fix me right up.'

"We thought little of the event," Ralph goes on, "and we returned to the inn. After a glorious dinner, we retired to the room we shared and went to bed. That was my last restful night, George, for as we descended from our room the next morning, we found the inn a hubbub of excitement—and fear.

"The lobby of the inn was full of people. 'How horrible!' they were saying. 'Perhaps next time it will be one of *us!*'

"'What's all the commotion about?' you asked the desk clerk, remember, George?

"'Oh, it is terrible,' he told you. 'This morning the innkeeper found one of his dogs torn to shreds! The townspeople think it is the work of a werewolf! Oh, why are we plagued like this?'

"'A werewolf?' you said, and laughed. 'Why, that's nonsense!' You always were a supremely rational type, George.

"'Not nonsense, Herr Doktor,' replied the desk clerk. 'It has happened before! Come, I will explain.' He drew the two of us into a quiet corner of his office. 'The woods surrounding this village are infested with a wild plant called wolfsbane,' he told us. 'Legend has it that anyone who touches it will turn into a wolf on the night of the full moon. *Last night the moon was full!*'

"The desk clerk took out a large, dusty

book to show us. 'See, here is a picture of the plant of which I speak. We have not destroyed it because no one will go near it.'

"Well, George, I gulped very hard when I saw the picture. It was the same plant I had scratched myself on! I was beginning to have a very sick feeling.

"The desk clerk was still talking, but I hardly heard him. 'Many times before this has occurred, Herr Doktor,' he was telling you. Then he looked at me. 'Herr Doktor,' he said, 'is something wrong with your friend? He does not look well.'

"'Huh?' you said. 'Oh, Ralph, you mean? Why, I guess your story has upset him. I'm sure he'll be all right.'

"I climbed the stairs to our room, George, in a trance. Droplets of cold sweat beaded my body. Could it be? *I had to know!*

"I tore the room apart. I looked everywhere, searched everything, hunting for something that could connect me with that dog's death. I found nothing—until I picked up my trench coat. Nothing there. But wait, what was this? A reddish stain . . . like . . . like *blood!* And short, curly hairs! *Dog's hair!* Oh, no! My voice was shouting in my head, 'This means *I am a werewolf! I am! I am!*'

"I had to keep calm, George. I had to think. What to do? Remove the stains, that was it! Wash them away!

"You came into the room as I was bending over the sink, George, remember? 'Ralph!' you said in surprise. 'What are you doing?'

"I barely recovered myself. 'Wha—?' I stammered. 'Oh, er, yes . . . yes, George, I'm fine. Just washing some—er—dirt off my coat.'

"You said nothing, George. But you looked at me. I saw you looking at me.

"For a moment I thought you knew. But you said nothing, and I breathed easier. We left for London that afternoon. We were in the car, remember? And you said, 'We'll stop off at Brussels and Paris for a while, eh, Ralph? Ought to be in London in about two weeks.'

"I was too unnerved to do anything but agree weakly. So off we went.

"But you were wrong, George. In two weeks we had only reached Paris. Gay, exciting Paris. The thrilling, pulsating night life, coupled with the wine and the carefree atmosphere, induced us to prolong our stay.

"My fears had almost disappeared—almost, but not quite: Several nights later a raging werewolf roamed the streets of Paris.

"I awoke the next day to face the shocking facts of the glaring morning headlines: 'YOUNG WOMAN BRUTALLY SLAIN! . . . Body mutilated as if attacked by a wild animal! . . . one shoe missing . . .'

"'One shoe,' I said to myself. 'One shoe.' Feverishly I began to tear apart the hotel room, just as I had in the village inn, looking for evidence of the previous night. Luckily you were out, George, so I could do my demonic work in peace. I went through everything. And then I found it: a red high-heeled shoe. There was blood on it.

"I quickly dressed and disposed of the shoe by throwing it down an incinerator chute. When I returned to our room, George, you were there.

"'George,' I begged you, 'I want to leave Paris right away! We've been here long enough! I don't want to stay any longer!'

"'Why, Ralph!' you said. 'I thought you were having a good time. But if you want to leave, it's okay by me.'

"We packed and left. As our car sped toward the coast of France, I fought to keep from being engulfed by the fear that seethed within me. 'Now I *know*,' I said to myself bitterly. 'I know for sure! But what can I do? How can I stop myself? *How* can I stop? Maybe when I'm out of this country . . . or off the Continent, maybe then I'll be all right again.' I hardly dared to hope, but I was in such a panic I wanted it to be true.

"At Le Havre, we had to wait till the following day before boarding a ship to cross the channel to England. But even with Paris far behind, I was afraid. London was smothered in fog when we arrived that night. Mist glistened on the pavements of the quiet streets.

"'Well, Ralph,' you told me, 'I've booked passage for us on the *Queen*. We leave for home next month. That's not too long to wait, is it?'

"I was stunned, George. But what could I say? 'Next month?' I repeated, swallowing hard. 'Er, no . . . no, George, that's not too long.' But inside I was dying.

"Time inched its way across the calendar, and the weeks passed quietly . . . quietly, until a few days before we were to sail. For it was a night of the full moon . . . and the werewolf stalked again!

"And as usual, the same shocking fear coursed through me as I learned of the terrible incident the following morning. I heard it on the radio: 'Early this morning police found the horribly torn and mutilated body of Anthony Essex, bellboy of the London Square Hotel. Police are speculating on the theory that this may be the work of another Jack the Ripper! The bellboy was still in his uniform when found, and only his hat is missing. No clues have—' I turned off the radio. I'd heard enough.

"I dreaded what I knew I would find—proof once again that I had killed. I found it in my coat pocket: the crumpled, bloodstained bellboy's hat."

At last Ralph has finished his story. He heaves a tremendous sigh and sits up on the couch. "And that's it, George," he says. "We sailed several days later and docked here in New York about three weeks ago. Now you know why I've come to you, George. This is the night of the full moon . . . and I'm terrified!"

George smooths down his hair and lights a cigarette. "You should have told me this before, Ralph," he says. "But it's not too late. You see, this is all in your mind. It's impossible for anyone to physically turn into a wolf. You merely *think* that!"

"I . . . I do?" says Ralph, rubbing his chin thoughtfully.

"Certainly," replies George. "The belief that people can assume the appearance and characteristics of a wolf is an ancient one. But believe me, it is impossible. True, tales of lycanthropy occur even today in savage or semicivilized races, but it is now regarded as a form of insanity. And it is characterized by abnormal desires for certain foods, including human flesh."

"You—you're saying I'm—I'm *not* a werewolf?" asks Ralph, trying to absorb all this in-

formation. "But—but that I'm—I'm *insane?*"

"Ralph, my boy," says George with a smile, "you're not a werewolf. And you're not insane."

"George . . . I don't . . . I don't understand. I—"

"Look out the window!" says George, drawing the curtains open with a flourish. "Does the moon have any effect on you? Does it? *Does it?*"

"N-no, George! I feel perfectly normal, but

. . . but—" Ralph paces the room, trying to understand. "What about the evidence, George? What about the bellboy's hat, the woman's shoe? Can you explain away the dog's blood smears on my coat? Can you?"

"Yes," says George. "Yes, I can. It would have been simple for someone to plant the shoe, the hat, for you to find. Simple if someone were close to you, someone able to get and wear your coat. Someone, perhaps, who shared your room."

"Wha-what?" stutters Ralph uncomprehendingly. "Someone—close? *George!* You mean—"

"Yes, Ralph, yes! I'm the werewolf! I killed those people! I did it!" George, suddenly slavering like a mad animal, fangs dripping in anticipation, leaps upon his friend Ralph with the power of a hundred men. *"And now I'm going to kill you!"* he shrieks in a brutal voice.

The horrified scream of a man in the agonies of death pierces the night's stillness. Above the wet, deserted street the full moon is the only witness. . . .

Well, kiddies, wasn't that perfectly delicious? I cooked it up myself, with just a pinch of wolfsbane for flavor.

Wait—what's that floating in the pot? Ecch! Looks kind of slimy to me. Oh well, a little extra . . . protein . . . never hurt anyone.

And for some music to enrich our dining experience, let's go right to the next story. . . .

 *And now, boils and ghouls, we've come to my masterpiece of musical morbidity. This story really should be accompanied by <u>sax and violins</u>. Get it? Sax and violins? Well, ahem, I guess I better not <u>string</u> you along anymore. So let's take it from the top—the*

CONCERTO FOR VIOLIN
AND WEREWOLF

Sacha Barak, the famed concert violinist, clutched his precious Stradivarius protectively to his breast and cursed softly to himself as the old coach rumbled and bumped through the Rumanian countryside.

"Blast!" he muttered. "These confounded Transylvanian highways are even worse than I remember them. If it weren't to see Vasile Iorga, I would never even *attempt* such a journey!" He held his hundred-eighty-thousand-dollar instrument closer.

Sacha leaned out the window and shouted at the driver, who remained sullen and mute. "Slow down, you fool! Do you want to get us

both killed?" But on they charged.

At last the creaking, groaning coach arrived in Brudja. It was a desolate, forbidding place. "No wonder they don't pave the roads around here," thought Sacha. "Why would anyone ever want to come?"

And when he finally found Vasile Iorga's ancient house on the edge of town, he was feeling even sorrier that he'd made the journey. For his old teacher, the man he'd dreamed of visiting for so long, didn't recognize him.

"Who are you? What do you want?" he quavered, peering at Sacha.

"Maestro! It's your old pupil Sacha! Sacha Barak! I've come so far to see you! Don't you remember me?"

Sacha almost wept as he looked at the face of his teacher, a face that had once been handsome and powerful and noble, but now was withered and toothless, with faded, watery eyes. Vasile was a mere shell of the strict, stern maestro Sacha had so long revered.

"Forgive me, Sacha," said Vasile Iorga, recognizing his student at last. "I do not see as well as I used to! How good of you to remember."

"As if I could ever forget the man who recognized my talent when I was but a child—and taught me all I know."

Suddenly Sacha noticed the old man stiffen . . . saw his face grow gray and his eyes fill with terror.

"Sacha!" cried the old man. "You should never have come to visit me here in Brudja! It is dangerous!"

"Dangerous?" echoed Sacha in confusion. "Why, Maestro?"

The old man looked around uneasily, and then stared at his former pupil. "Don't you remember, Sacha?" he whispered. "This is werewolf country! Don't you recall the incident that took place almost twenty years ago when I was living in Chisasi and you used to come for lessons?"

"How could I?" said Sacha, a bit annoyed. "So many things have happened since then. What incident?"

"Don't you remember that young couple?" replied the teacher. "They'd driven here from Budapest, impulsively risking a tour through the Transylvanian Alps. The rugged road between Chisasi and Brudja had proved too much for their motorcar.

"They had stopped the car, and the young man had gotten out to see what the trouble was. The woman stayed in the car, shivering in the freezing night air.

"The young man slid underneath the car to have a look. A full moon had risen, filtering through the gnarled old trees, and an ominous silence enveloped the lonely surrounding countryside. A rustling of nearby brambles caused the woman to turn her head, and what she saw brought a soul-piercing scream from her throat.

"It was a werewolf. It sprang upon the young woman, sinking its razor-sharp fangs into her soft white flesh, while her husband scrambled from beneath the car. 'Marta!' he cried.

"As the young man came at the slobbering, snarling, bloodthirsty werewolf, it fled. Shaking with horror, he flung his lantern after the fleeing beast. The lantern shattered against a tree trunk, bursting into flame, and he saw, by the sudden light, his wife's arm dangling from the werewolf's drooling mouth.

"Don't you remember, Sacha?" said the agitated old teacher. "You heard the screams . . . the growls . . . the commotion outside. You wanted to go. 'Never mind, Sacha,' I told you. 'Your debut is only two weeks off. We must practice. It is nothing! Get back to your music stand!'

" 'But, Maestro!' you begged me. 'There must be something wrong! Look! Men running . . . with lanterns!' "

The old man grabbed his former student by the shoulders and looked pleadingly into his eyes. "Don't you remember the woman lying beside the car, her eyes staring, her face ashen? And her husband listening in horror to the doctor telling him she was dead? 'Maestro!' you cried. 'What happened to her?'

"'Come away, Sacha,' I said, pulling you home. 'Come away.'"

The old teacher finished his story with a sigh. Sacha noticed that he was shaking and covered with sweat, and his toothless old mouth quivered. "Don't you remember?" asked the exhausted old man.

"Oh, yes!" replied the famous violinist. "Of course, Maestro. I do remember. But the explanation of the incident was simple enough. The woods are full of wolves! They've been known to attack a man . . ."

"There have been more incidents, Sacha," interrupted the teacher. "Here! Read this newspaper sent to me from Bucharest!" He thrust the paper toward Sacha.

"Do you expect me to believe there is a werewolf here in Brudja?" scoffed Sacha.

"I ask you to believe *this!* See the date? Nearly two months ago! Read," urged Vasile.

Reluctantly Sacha began reading aloud from the newspaper: "'A Bucharest man paid with his life last night when he ignored the warning to stay away from the Transylvanian town of Brudja. There was a full moon, and his body, stripped of flesh, was found . . .'"

The old man was too agitated to let him finish. He pointed a gnarled finger at the article. "There was a full moon, Sacha!" he cried. "A lycanthropic moon! In two days there'll be another! I beg of you. *Do not stay in Brudja!*"

"Nonsense, Maestro," said the violinist in irritation. "I am as safe here as you are. If I am not welcome in your home, I will go to the inn. But I will not be frightened into leaving Brudja!"

The old maestro shrugged his shoulders. "You always were stubborn, Sacha. And I do want you to stay. It's just that, at this time of the month ... a *stranger* in town ... well, promise me you'll keep your bedroom windows and door locked."

"Of course, Maestro," said Sacha lightly. "I know how to take care of myself. Look." He opened his suitcase and took out a large revolver. "I carry it to protect myself and my Stradivarius."

"A Stradivarius!" exclaimed the teacher. "A genuine Stradivarius! Let me see!" Old Vasile opened Sacha's violin case and drew forth the Stradivarius. He fondled it reverently as Sacha stared at his gun.

"If I remember it right, Maestro," Sacha mused, "legend has it that only a silver bullet can kill a werewolf."

"Beautiful," rhapsodized Vasile, so entranced by the instrument that he did not hear Sacha. "Beautiful." Then he realized what he had heard Sacha saying. "Eh? What are you thinking?" he asked in alarm.

"I'm thinking about killing me a werewolf, Vasile. Do you have an iron kettle I may use to melt down some silver?"

"Don't be a fool, Sacha!" said the old man. "Why risk your life?"

"I am no fool, Maestro! Think of the publicity I will receive. Headlines in all the papers throughout Europe! FAMED VIOLINIST FREES ROMANY TOWN OF RAMPAGING WEREWOLF! You see, Vasile, there's more to success than mere genius! Even I must have publicity. So stop worrying about me. Tell you what. You may play my Stradivarius as long as I stay here. There! Now get me that kettle . . ."

Sacha spent the next few hours in the cellar, melting down silver coins and pouring the molten silver into a mold he'd made by pressing the slug from an ordinary bullet into moist earth. And as he worked, the strains of a sad gypsy air filtered down from the parlor.

"Hmmm," Sacha said to himself as he worked. "The old boy can still play."

When the silver slugs were cooled, Sacha removed the lead slugs from the regular bullets and replaced the silver ones in the steel jackets. He went upstairs, filled the chambers of his revolver with his handiwork, and placed the gun in his overcoat pocket.

"There, Maestro!" he said triumphantly. "Now I'm ready for the werewolf of Brudja!"

But Vasile hardly heard him, so in love was he with the Stradivarius. "Such tone, Sacha!" he said. "Such mellow sounds come from this glorious instrument!"

The next morning, even though the old maestro warned him against it, Sacha walked into town. The sun beat down on the market-place, but the warmth it brought was not enough to offset the cold, suspicious stares of the townsfolk.

"Hmmm," thought Sacha. "Not a friendly face among them. The way they look at me, you'd think I was the werewolf."

But there was more than suspicion in the townspeople's stares. Sacha seemed to sense a certain tenseness—even hostility. He plunged his hand into his overcoat pockets, feeling for the reassuring steel of his revolver. The pockets were empty.

"My gun!" he choked. "It's gone!"

He returned at once to Vasile Iorga's house. "I thought it was accidental that someone jostled me when I first entered the marketplace," he said to his old teacher. "But now I realize that *he* must have stolen my gun. Do you know what that *means,* Vasile? One of your townspeople is the werewolf!"

The old man looked grave. "Now that your gun is gone," he said, "perhaps you will leave!"

Sacha stared at his toothless maestro. "Wait a minute!" he exclaimed. "How did anyone know I had a gun? How did they know it was loaded with silver bullets? How could they? Vasile! *You* . . ."

"Yes, Sacha!" said the old man. "It was I! I took the gun from your pocket and threw it down the well! It was only because I am afraid for you . . ." The old man began to cry. "I did it for your own good, Sacha!" he blubbered.

"Now you are angry at me!"

"Angry at you? No, Maestro," said Sacha. "I am touched by your concern for my safety. But I have no intention of leaving Brudja!"

That night a gibbous moon, not quite full, bathed the old maestro's house in a cold pale light. Inside, Sacha scanned a newspaper while Vasile played the Stradivarius.

"Why, this is last month's *Bucharest Journal,* Vasile, and it came today," remarked Sacha.

"The mail is slow coming to Brudja, Sacha," the maestro explained. "You can understand."

Sacha was well into the paper before a report caught his eye. He leaped up with a start. "Vasile! Listen to this! 'There was a full moon last night when five persons from Chisasi became drunk while celebrating a wedding anniversary and wandered into the ill-famed town of Brudja. . . . A search party found the five bodies the next day outside the town. They had all been stripped of their flesh. . . . Bare skeletons . . . Unidentifiable . . .'"

"Yes, Sacha," said the old man sadly. "That happened last month. You see, it has happened so many times to so many hundreds of poor unfortunate people over the years, that we here in Brudja are no longer shocked by it." He played a few haunting notes on the beautiful violin.

"I recall something I read on my last concert tour, Vasile," said Sacha. "I wonder ... hmmm. Of course! How stupid of me! Tomorrow I am going into Chisasi for another gun."

Early the next morning Sacha Barak, the famed violinist, walked the seven miles to Chisasi in order to purchase the gun and bullets he needed. He carried his empty violin case.

"I should have guessed!" he berated himself as he trudged along. "Well, tonight the moon will be full, and I will be waiting for them ... in the marketplace."

It was past noon when he returned to Vasile's home. He grinned confidentially as he showed the old man the gun he'd bought.

"Tonight," he said, "I will go into town carrying my violin case—and who would suspect it conceals a gun?"

"No one!" agreed his teacher. "Of course!"

The rest of the afternoon was spent in the cellar, carefully molding bullets from molten silver. And when twilight was beginning to shroud the town, Sacha returned to the parlor with his silver ammunition. He loaded his gun and replaced it in the violin case.

"There!" he said. "Done! And now—" He turned to his teacher. "Good heavens, Vasile. Don't you ever tire of playing the violin?"

"Not this one, Sacha! Not a Stradivarius! Besides, you said I could play it while you stayed." And on and on he played.

Sacha rested in his room, waiting for the night, listening to the lilting strains of the violin. Suddenly he felt Vasile's hands shaking him.

"It's almost time, Sacha!" Vasile was saying. "The moon is almost full! Come, let us go!"

"Us?" said Sacha, sitting up. "No sir, old man. You're staying here. You told me yourself it would be dangerous."

But because Vasile insisted on coming with Sacha, they walked into town together. The moon cast an eerie glow upon the cobblestone streets. The marketplace was deserted, yet Sacha was aware of a frightening presence . . . something he could feel only instinctively. The

weight of the weapon in the violin case com-
forted him.

And then, slowly, the frightening presence
made itself known. The townspeople ... all of
the population of Brudja ... began to appear.
From alleys and doorways and deep shadows
they came toward Sacha and Vasile.

And as they came Sacha could see their red
eyes glowing in the full moonlight, and the hair
bristling on their faces, and their gleaming
white fangs. He could see their snarling, drooling werewolf faces. And then he began to
laugh.

"I *knew* I was right!" he said, fumbling with the latches of his violin case. "When I read in the paper that five bodies were stripped of their flesh, I knew there had to be more than one werewolf!

"And then I remembered a story I'd read on my last concert tour—a story called 'Midnight Mess' about a town populated by vampires! And I knew! I knew then that Brudja was a town of werewolves. And that I'd have to be ready for you . . ."

The snarling, howling beasts were almost upon him now, and their howling sounded like laughter too. Sacha reached inside his open violin case.

"Well, I *am* ready for you!" he shouted. "All of you! Because I've got a gun . . . loaded with silver bullets! Not just any gun! A Thompson submachine gun! I'm ready for . . . for . . . *Good lord!*"

Sacha's laughter stopped abruptly as the beasts sprang upon him. For there was no submachine gun in his violin case—only a useless old Stradivarius. And as flashing teeth tore into him he heard his old maestro's voice:

"Careful of the violin!" it screeched. "And save some soft parts for a toothless old werewolf. Remember, I brought him! I fixed things! I took out the gun . . ."

Well, kiddies, let that be a <u>lesson</u> to you: don't <u>fiddle</u> around with werewolves or you might end up listening to the "Funeral March"! If Sacha had only had a better memory, he would have remembered that the first song his old maestro had taught him was "The Moonlight Sonata."

And now it's time to stop reading and go to bed. But first look out your window and see if there's a full moon tonight. If there is, you'll want to be sure to get out your comb. It's such a drag when your face fur gets all matted, don't you agree?

G'night!